Max got a new Speed Demon sled for Christmas.

W9-CEO-378

He wanted to ride down Rocket Run.

"Oh no, Max," said Max's older sister, Ruby.
"Rocket Run is for big bunnies," said Louise.

Ruby took Max to Bunny Hill.
She hopped onto the back of his sled.
"One, two, three. Whee!" yelled Ruby.

They went down the hill very slowly.
"Faster," said Max.

They climbed to the top of Bunny Hill.
"This time I'll give you a big push," said Ruby.
"One, two, three. Whee!" yelled Ruby.

Max went down the hill very slowly.
"Faster," said Max.

Max climbed to the top of Bunny Hill.
"This time Louise and I will push you," said Ruby.
"One, two, three. Whee!" yelled Ruby and Louise together.

Max went down the hill very slowly.
"Faster," said Max.
He still wanted to ride down Rocket Run.

"Oh no, Max," said Ruby.
"Rocket Run is for big bunnies," said Louise.

Ruby, Louise and Max walked to Rocket Run.
Big bunnies were going down the hill very fast.

Ruby and Louise were scared.

"Still want to go?" asked Ruby.
"Sure…if you do," said Louise.

"We can do it," said Ruby.
"Of course we can," said Louise.

"Bunny Scouts are brave and true.
When a job must be done, what do we do?
Hop to it!" said Ruby and Louise together.

Ruby and Louise were ready for Rocket Run.
But their toboggan was missing!

Max was missing too!
But his Speed Demon sled was still there.

Ruby and Louise looked down Rocket Run.
Max was racing down the hill on their toboggan!
"Faster!" yelled Max.

Ruby and Louise hopped on Max's Speed Demon sled.
They raced down the hill after Max.

Max hit a big bump.
He flew through the air.

Ruby and Louise hit a big bump.
They flew through the air.

Everyone landed in a big pile of snow.

"Max. Are you all right?" asked Ruby.

"Faster!" yelled Max.